Pilgrim's Bay

The author would like to send special thanks to the editors and staff at the following publications for taking time to read and publish his writing:

The Adirondack Review
Fluid Magazine
Me Three
Circle Magazine
Cellar Door
Prose Ax
WriteGallery
David Coyote's Den
East of the Web
Temenos
BloodLotus

Other books by k.j. stevens

<u>A Better Place</u>

<u>Infidelity</u>

<u>Dead Bunnies</u>

Pilgrim's Bay

by k.j. stevens

crooked steeple press
7868 smith road
alpena, michigan 49707

Pilgrim's Bay © 2007 by k.j. stevens

This is a work of fiction.

Cover art by Rita L. Stevens
www.ritastevens.com

✷

~ For Mom and Dad ~

Contents

July 5th, 2007
9:03 pm

The thunder is booming all around. Lightning flashes. Day is giving way to night. And I'm still here. Upstairs in the old house. My perch above the wide green field where deer and turkeys fatten up. My bird's eye view of the cemetery. Where people come to visit, pay respects, gather thoughts, and cry. But it is also a place to maintain a connectedness. To gain perspective. To stay true.

It is hard staying on this path. The one less traveled by. But look at us. How far we've come. How much stronger we are. Seems like we will be walking together a long, long while. Just me and you. Hand in hand. Down the old gravel road. Knowing full well that when the end does come up to meet us, we'll simply keep on keepin' on...

Best,

~ k.j.

the place

We live in Pilgrim's Bay. Our small town. With narrow, weather-beaten roads. Broken concrete. Crumbling asphalt. Sunken cobblestones. Streets, avenues, trails. And bridges. All of them leading to, from, and across Lake Huron, the Pilgrim's Bay River, and their streams. Along these roads stand two-hundred year old houses with peeling paint, broken shingles and wooden floors that creak and sigh. Our people watch the world pass by through large tired windows. Dirty glass panes that have been melting slowly. Invisibly over time. So that they've become thicker at the bottom than at the top. A lot like the people living in these houses. Shuffling their heavy feet. Taking for granted the solid foundations beneath them.

Pilgrim's Bay feels safe. Too safe. Never had a murder. Don't have much crime. We are quiet folks, living quiet lives in a lakeshore town. Once, we were loggers. Now, we work in the steel mill. The paper plant. On the boats, or in the quarry. But some of us don't work at all. We get by on unemployment. Social security. Handouts. And the land.

The Pilgrim's Bay River brings ships in and sends ships out. Lake Huron rises and falls. Works with the river moving people, goods, our lives, as best it can. Those things it cannot handle, it sinks. And the deep cold water consumes.

Besides shipwrecks, the only time Pilgrim's Bay has made headlines was when *Newsday* listed it as one of the top ten places to live. If you're an alcoholic. But I'm not sure we're all drunks. I think our headlining has to do with the churches we've forgotten. The gods we've lost. The lives we've taken for granted. And the way we've given up on love.

<u>friends</u>

Me, Jake, and Kali meet up day-after-day. At Sammy's Bar. Five dollar pitchers from ten to midnight. Pearl Jam. The Doors. Janis Joplin on the jukebox. There are other artists, but we don't care. We know what we like. And we like where we are. At Sammy's Bar. In a ratty old booth. Drinking shots and beer after beer.

"Suckers are runnin' in Polack Creek," Jake says. Elbows on the table. Both hands on his beer.

Kali's playing with her hair. Smelling good. Like she's just showered. And I am doing my best to take her all in. Without letting myself get taken back in.

"Jake, why do you say it like that?" she asks.

"Like what?"

"Why do you have to say *Polack*?"

She takes a drink. Lights a cigarette.

"I call it *Polack* because that's its goddamned name."

Kali sucks hard at the cigarette. Blows smoke with fury.

"And that too," she says. "You and all your *goddamns*. Ignorance. That's what it is."

I've been waiting for this. For Kali to introduce us to the knowledge she's gaining from attending PBCC. Pilgrim's Bay Community College. Since we've broken apart, she's been attending classes three days a week. It's so she can learn about life, she says. The good. The bad. The right and wrong. But I think Kali is moving through life like the rest of us. Biding time on the surface. Immersed in daily distractions. So that we are not tempted to go deep. To the places where we keep things hidden. Like anchors and bells, boat motors and old cars. Preserved by cold water. Made into houses for fish.

"*Polack* is a derogatory term, Jake."

Jake looks at me. Slowly shakes his head in disgust. We've always called it Polack Creek because that's what the sign's always said. POLACK CREEK. In big block letters. Carved into a thick wooden board. Stuck deep into the ground near the culvert since we were kids. Put there by Bob Donakowski. A big, burly foundry worker who made his fortune playing the Michigan lottery. Hitting it big. Millions and millions. So that he was able to buy as much property as he could along Misery Bay. So that it could never be developed. Zoned for housing. Changed. And that was just fine by me and Jake as it was one of our favorite places to fish.

"Kali," I say, "don't go off on Jake. We're not here for anything, but *this*."

I raise my glass for a toast.

Kali smiles.

"And what is *this*, Aden?"

"This is *us*. Friends in a booth. Drinking."

"Ah yes," Kali says. "Once again, I have the pleasure of watching the boys drown their sorrows."

"I'm not a boy," Jake snaps. "And I'm not drowning

sorrows."

He raises his glass to mine.

"A toast!" he shouts.

Reluctantly, Kali raises her glass to ours. Jake flashes his crooked smile.

"To ignorant Poles everywhere!" he hollers.

Jake and I race to the bottom. Slam our glasses to the table. Kali lowers hers. Moves it around in big wet circles. She turns to face me. But our eyes do not meet. She sees through me. Toward the jukebox. And blows smoke at dirty ceiling tiles. I am used to this. Her disappointment. And the solid knot of regret that tightens and burns in my gut. It is my punishment. For leaving her. For not saving us. For our loss. And slowly, it is killing me.

She leans forward so that her hair brushes the table.

"Jake, you do realize that *you're* a Polack, don't you?"

"Sure do!" he beams.

I know I shouldn't. But the beer has reached my belly. Soaked the knot. Entered my bloodstream. And begun its run. Out of spite, or resentment, or the hope that I'll get some reaction, I decide to add a little more fuel to the fire.

"I'll second that!" I shout. "Jake, you are thee finest *goddamned* Polack I know!"

Jake winks.

"You're not so bad yourself," he says. "But there'll be no

more Polacks and no more goddamns. We don't want to disappoint Kali."

He shakes his finger at the ceiling.

"And we mustn't forget. The big man *is* watching."

Kali snubs her cigarette in the ashtray. Twirls her fingers in her hair. And it looks as though we might lose her. She is staring off into the smoky air. Biting her lip. Tapping her foot. Watching people as they come into the bar.

I take one more stab.

"Jake and God have a lot in common," I say.

She sighs, turns toward me.

"Something tells me I shouldn't ask, but I will anyway. What is it that Jake and God have in common?"

Jake leans forward.

"We're both carpenters!" he shouts, and he pounds his fist on the table. But Kali doesn't flinch.

"Carpenters, I say!"

Jake *is* a carpenter. In fact, he's so good at it that instead of going to college after high school, or taking over his old man's shoe store, he's built a workshop, bought a van, filled it with wood and tools, and became known as the town's very own *Woodwork on Wheels*.

I raise my glass. Jake raises his. We wait for Kali to raise hers, but she snubs us.

"To Jake and God!" I toast. "Creators both!"

"It's a shame," Jake says. "Nobody giving a shit about God no more. A damned shame. People got distractions. And they're moving farther away from God every day. TV and movies. Clothes and cars. Mass-produced kitchen cabinets and futons made in Taiwan. Goddamned people. Everyone's losing God..."

He stops suddenly. Takes a deep breath.

"When's the last time you went to church?" Kali asks.

"The van, the wood, and Polack Creek. Those are *my* church."

He grabs the pitcher. Fills our glasses. And we are quiet for a time with our thoughts and our drinking. Jake sits and smiles into the round flickering light above our booth. Kali sparks up another cigarette. I sip my beer, breathe the dirty air, but I feel good. We are one pitcher into the night, Eddie Vedder sings that he's still *Alive*, and I'm glancing at a blonde who's playing pool.

Her hair is straight and shoulder length. Her body is slender, but full of shape and curve. Her cheeks are dimpled when she smiles, and she's smiling a lot. Twice so far, I think she's smiled at me.

"That dame's a scorcher," Jake says, his attention gone from booth light to blonde.

Kali takes a long drag. Exhales slowly. Through her nose.

"A dame? Dammit Jake, you're sick. A sick little boy."

I take my eyes off the blonde and chime in.

"Jake's not sick. He's just gone from looking at one light to looking at another."

Jake nods toward the blonde.

"And, *Miss Kali*, I think you forget one crucial detail."

"What's that?" she asks.

"That it's the big carpenter upstairs that's made that little angel."

He laughs and drinks. Condensation beads. Trickles down his glass. Kali looks at me. And finally, we have a rare moment when our eyes wander into each other. And I get lost in dark chocolate pools. Moments shared. Secrets known. The sorrow and pity. Desire and resentment. Memory and loss. She is the place I once belonged. A faint breath of deja-vu that stirs everything so that there's nothing I can do but break the gaze. Look away. And forget. Because I cannot go back. And be inside her again.

I stand. Dig into my pockets for change.

"What are you doing?" she asks.

"Going to the jukebox."

Jake tops our glasses. Empties the pitcher. Kali rises. Takes it from him. Glides away to the bar. Wispy smoke follows in her wake.

"Any requests?" I shout after her.

She turns. Smiles. Flips me the bird.

✿

Sammy's is usually dead. But tonight there are extra bodies. College kids wearing college sweatshirts and college hats. Central Michigan University. Albion. U of M. Even some good old PBCC. I can't imagine why they've all come to Sammy's. There are other places closer to where they're from. Clubs with hips shaking and bodies rocking to pounding bass. Cover-charging, three-level joints serving Jell-O-shots in plastic cups, or watered down booze in test tubes. All of it sold by beautiful waiters and waitresses flirting for dollars. At the jukebox in front of me, two girls are flipping through music. Long dark hair pulled into pony tails. Stinking of perfume. Wearing identical red sweatshirts.

"This place has awful music," one says. "It's so *old*! The Doors? Janis Joplin?"

"It's shit! That's what it is," the other says. "The most recent thing they have is Pearl Jam. Didn't their lead singer shoot himself like ten years ago?"

"If not, he should have."

I move closer to them, jingling change.

"Excuse me. Can I squeeze in there and play some music?"

They crane their necks to look at me.

Very pretty girls. Experts at camouflage and concealment. Made up nice with fake tans, Revlon and

Maybelline. They scowl at me then smile at each other.

"Excuse *us*," one says. "That's what *we're* trying to do. Wait your turn."

They turn back to the jukebox. I stand there. Steaming. Jake appears at my side. Looks at the girls. Gives me an elbow and a wink. Hands me an icy mug of beer.

"What's taking so long?" he asks.

"Waiting for these young ladies," I say. "They seem to be having a most difficult time with their music selections."

"Most difficult?" Jake asks.

"Yes. Most difficult."

The girls turn and look at us. On the front of their shirts it says, *Success is getting IT. Greeks get IT.* Me and Jake move closer to them. Squint at the writing on their chests. They back away.

"You really think they get it, Jake?"

He gulps his beer. Burps. Smiles wide.

"Sure, they do! All these Greek goddesses get it. A lot!"

The girls shove through us and walk away.

Jake takes my change. Puts it in the jukebox. Punches in the numbers. We've been here so many times that we have the music memorized.

#1005—Black by Pearl Jam

#1070— Take a Little Piece of my Heart by Janis Joplin

#0771— People Are Strange by The Doors

Kali's back at the booth. Pouring beer. Me and Jake move through the crowd toward her. There is smoke. Laughter. Beer everywhere. I bump and brush against bodies and I feel like I'm losing bits and pieces of myself to everyone around me. It's a familiar feeling. Quick like lightning, but intimate and lasting all the same.

"Have fun flirting?" Kali asks.

I sit next to her.

"Those were a couple of grade-A bitches. Not like you, Kali. You're a nice girl."

Jake stretches out in the booth. Puts his feet up and yawns.

"Kali's not nice," he says.

"That's right," Kali adds.

She slides over on the booth seat. Moves away from me.

"I'm a bitch, too. I just haven't persuaded anyone I'm bitchy enough for them."

I lean forward. Rest my elbows on the table. Look into my glass. Stare into the beer until a foamy face appears. Elongated head. Hollow eyes. A wide grin. And I think about how it won't be long before I'm to the bottom again. And suddenly, I can feel her energy. Kali. As far away from me as she can get. But radiating heat. Warming me. And smelling so damn good that all I want to do is bury my face in her hair and breathe. And hold her and stay that way until the day I die. So, I lift the glass. Take a long drink. Wash it away. Send it down deep. Until it reaches the knot and drowns.

"What about your little angel at the pool table?" Kali asks. "I bet *she's* the real deal. Pretty, funny *and* smart."

"Bet she's a goddamned genius."

Jake says this as he slides his glass toward me, nodding at the pitcher.

"A goddamned genius. Like one of those PBCC girls."

I top off our glasses, but stay silent. Kali says nothing. Jake talks more about the sucker run. He'll go tonight after the bar and shine the water, he says. He's got a hard hat and it's got a flashlight mounted on top. He will walk out onto the end of the big culvert. Lean over the edge. Steady himself. And he will wait five minutes in the dark. Listen to the crickets and frogs and the sound of deer navigating the swamp. Then he'll turn on the flashlight and hope for a dying run. Because if they're running steady at night, they won't run long. Just some quick lovin', he says. And the more Jake talks, the more I'm convinced that the swimming upstream has more to do with being together than it does with reproduction, life, and carrying on the species. The truth, Jake says, is that fish love like men. They fight upstream for nothing. Only to get beaten and die in the end.

Eddie Vedder croons through the speaker above our booth, "*...I take a walk outside, I'm surrounded by some kids at* *play. I can feel their laughter, so why do I sear?"*

Kali raises her glass.

"I'll drink to that!" she says. "To kids playing and souls searing."

I raise my glass.

"There aren't any souls searing."

Kali smiles.

"But kids *are* playing."

"Bullshit. Let's drink to something else."

"To fishing!" Jake shouts.

The three of us rattle glasses. Drink. Sip and spill. I look at the pool table. There isn't anyone playing. The blonde's gone to a corner. Is talking with her Greek, pony-tailed friends. And there are more Greeks too. Frat boys and sorority girls standing around everywhere. Drinking. Smoking. Making Sammy's feel like something else other than home.

"Wanna shoot pool?" Jake asks.

Kali glares.

"You boys and your games. Why can't we sit and talk?"

I shrug my shoulders and rise from the booth. My vision whirls. I try focusing on Jake as he carries the beer toward the pool table, but he looks like a different man. It's as if I've never seen him before. Dirty jeans covered in wood dust. Faded black shirt with the sleeves torn off. Steel-toed work boots dragging frayed leather laces. Leaving a trail of wood shavings behind. I feel like I'm lost in unfamiliar space. Moving around in someone else's body. Spending time with someone else's friends. Seeing everything for the first time. Again.

I guzzle my beer as I approach the pool table. Move to put quarters into the slots. But there are already some there. I look around at the Greeks. Most of them have their backs toward the table. Others look through me. The two girls in red sweatshirts glance my way and scowl.

Bar etiquette says I'm to wait for the person who has the quarters up, as they have control of the table.

"Is this an open table?" I ask, loud enough so everyone can hear.

One of the red-shirts turns toward me. Hisses like an angry cat.

"Does it *look* like anybody's playing?"

I shove the quarters into the table. Balls fall and rumble. The blonde steps away from her group.

"Those quarters are mine."

"I asked if the table was open."

"You didn't ask me. You stepped over here like you own the place and you took the table."

I look to Jake and Kali. Jake is smiling. Kali struggles to watch.

"Well, with the amount of time and money we spend here, we sorta do own the place."

I take a pool stick from the rack. Call to Jake and Kali. "Who wants to break?"

The blonde waits. I walk by her and start to rack the balls. Jake sidles up to her.

"I'm Jake. That's Kali. And *this*..." he says, shaking a finger at me, "is Aden."

She comes to me. Takes the stick away.

"I'm Maggie. My quarters. My table. I break."

Kali lights another cigarette. Jake walks to the bar. Orders a round of shots.

I rack the balls and I watch Maggie. She isn't wearing any makeup. Or at least, very little. She has pleasant green eyes. Thin lips. A fair complexion. There is something about her that strikes me. Makes me nervous. Self conscious. Aware. I center the balls, remove the rack, and I watch. Maggie leans over the table. Readies herself to break. And a silver cross falls out of her shirt. Dangles from a necklace. Spins and sparkles above the green felt.

"Kamikazees!" Jake cheers, as he hands each of us a shot. "How about a toast, Aden?"

The small glass feels big in my hand. The place buzzes and revolves around me. Beer mugs. Bar stools. Booths. And I am the center of my own dysfunctional universe. There's a long silent pause between jukebox songs, so I take a deep breath and I toast.

"To playing the game!"

I say it, but hear it too. A weak voice. Aiming farther than it can carry. I look around the place, searching. For a feeling. Recognition. Something new. And then I see myself in the mirror behind the bar. A boyish looking man. A red-nosed stranger. Heavy under the chin. Thicker at the bottom than at the top. With Maggie behind me. Moving toward me. The silver cross shining. Flickering in the dim light. As she touches it with her long, white fingers. Tucks it into her shirt. And I feel like I've seen her thousands of times.

Jake swears up and down that suckers are running in Polack Creek. That it's one of the most beautiful things a man can see. That by tomorrow or the next day, they'll have reached Indian Creek and he can't wait to do some spear-chuckin', he says. Fishing like the natives used to.

Kali laughs. Begins to relax. Steps out of the present and visits the past. Back to this place we belong. Sammy's Bar and Pilgrim's Bay. Drinking away at quiet desperation until it feels like contentment. Numbing reality so that the true, fragile lines of happiness are impossible to see.

Back at the table, I stare at the triangle of balls. Colors and numbers. Organization and form given to small spheres. Balls floating on the green sea. Waiting for the break.

My guts roll over. Arms and legs tingle. I look down at my shaking hands. The shape. The skin. The scars. They are

strange to me. And I'm trapped inside. Feeling like something
yet to be discovered.

We down more shots. Pitchers are filled. Emptied. We
consume the offerings. Sedate ourselves with distraction so that
whatever rises is kept down. Weighted. Anchored deep. Where
it belongs.

Maggie smells like a spring morning. Is close enough to
touch. To have and to hold.

"I'll let you break," she says. And it feels like she means
everything.

the drive

Light breaks through the window. Warms my face. Wakes me. And I linger. Between morning and night. Sleep and dream. In the hollow place. Where another night has gone and another day appears. I'm alive. But exhausted and empty.

The phone rings. I reach for it. Muster a half-hearted *hello?*

"You ready?"

It is Jake. Only two words, but I can tell he's energized.

"Ready for what?"

"For fishing!"

"It's too early."

"It's three."

Out of the corner of my eye, red clock digits flash. *12:00. 12:00. 12:00*

"Sorry, Jake. My clock says noon."

"Sure, flashing twelve like mine. The power went out last night. Whole damned town. One of the Greek chariots nailed a power pole."

I sit up. Blood pounds my temples.

"What?"

"Last night. Two of the sorority girls bit it."

"They dead?"

"Not yet. Intensive care, I guess."

I'm silent. Acid rolls my stomach. Rises to my throat. And burns.

"Where did they wreck?"

"Mann's Corner," Jake says.

I rise from bed. Sit. Stretch. So blood surges. Courses through muscle and tissue. Makes me want to fall back. Into the mattress. Cover up. Rest till I'm dead. But I stand. Stretch some more. And look out the window. There are turkeys and deer sharing the gray field across the road. Pecking. Grazing. Warming under the bright afternoon sun.

"I think I'm still drunk."

"No doubt," Jake says. "You and Miss PBCC didn't have enough sense to know when to say when. Both of you were piss drunk."

"How'd I get home?"

"You drove."

"How did Maggie get home?"

"She called a cab."

I close my eyes and try to remember, but all I see are pieces. Maggie's smile. The silver cross. Green felt. Pitchers of beer. Jake's wood shavings and sawdust. Kali's brown eyes.

"You're supposed to meet her at Sammy's tonight," Jake says. "After we're done fishing."

"I don't feel like fishing."

"Too bad. We made plans for the dam."

"We make a lot of plans."

"I know, but today, of all days, I'm holding you to it. Get

dressed and get your ass over here."

"But Jake..."

The line clicks dead.

☼

I load my fishing gear into the truck. Sense something in the air. Like snow. Growing in clouds. Or an ice storm creeping in. It is the change of seasons. The final push from winter to spring. But it is something deeper too. Heavy and solid that chills.

I start the truck. Turn on the radio. And I watch the turkeys and the deer move in the field as I listen to the news. As usual, Jake's details are skewed. The girls are not Greek. They are from Hillman. Minors. Drunk driving. Two girls out of control. Into a power pole. They weren't wearing seatbelts. The air bag was deployed. They were taken to the hospital. Treated and released. Now, they are in jail. And so the legend of Mann's Corner will grow.

When I roll the old Ford out onto the road, the turkeys take flight. Their big shadows shift and change shape as they pass over the deer, forgotten hay bales, and the uneven ground. It seems impossible that these big birds have entered the sky. That they are skimming over the cattails and willows that guard the swamp at the edge of the field. But they are. And they are quick. And graceful. As they disappear into the bush.

The deer pay no mind to the turkeys. Or to the truck, as I

pull away with the exhaust clanging and rumbling, tires sending stones and dirt into the air. Their white tails swish and ears twitch as they graze on sweet shoots, soft blades and new stems that spring has brought around. These deer have made it. Through hunting season. Through the harshest season. And they are safe. For now.

So it is a Sunday morning. I'm hungover. But I'm in the old Ford. Traveling a familiar road. Passing deer. Wide-open fields. And I can't help but thinking of Dad and our Sunday drives. The one thing that brought and kept us together after Mom died.

He would call me Saturday nights to confirm our trips for Sundays. When I wasn't home, when I was with Jake or Kali, or when I was alone and too drunk to care, Dad would leave messages on my answering machine.

"Aden, this is Dad. Just called to shoot the shit, but I imagine you're fishing with Jake, or doing something with Kali. Guess I'll see you tomorrow then. About six-thirty or so."

Dad. Calling to *shoot the shit*. Always reaching out. Without saying much. Talk about the weather. About chores. About how he couldn't sleep because of the neighbor's barking dog. Opossums in the garbage. Cats fighting in the dark. His voice deep and mechanical. Not a good phone voice. Not a good answering machine voice. Mom's the one that had the good voice. The one that did all the talking. Soft and soothing. She could talk for hours and people loved to listen. All I have left of Mom's voice is in memory. But Dad's is saved. In shoe boxes. Full of answering machine tapes. Under my bed.

Dad's messages brought me to his house every Sunday morning. To my old neighborhood. The place I grew up. The Ridge. Where the Pilgrim's Bay River cuts deep through clay and sand. Where Jake and I played. And where we learned to fish. The place we dug grubs. Caught grasshoppers. Trapped minnows. And picked night crawlers. Where we learned that anything could be used for bait. Marshmallows, hot dogs, strawberry taffy, or WD-40 sprayed on pieces of inner tube. It was where we learned to make strong, long-lasting bonfires for frying bluegills, steaming crayfish, and toasting S`mores. The place we learned to row and anchor. Swim. Tread water. And dive.

Jake still lives there. Part of The Ridge and part of the river. Living two houses down from the place I used to call home. The old two-story Victorian with the wraparound porch. The weathered swing. Where Dad swayed back-and-forth. In slow, easy motion. Sipping black coffee. Leafing through the pages of *Field & Stream*. Waiting for me. Every Sunday morning. Except for our last one. When I pulled into the driveway. Eyed the weeping willows. The wily rosebushes that Dad had let go to grow up around the railings and lattice work of the porch. And the swing was empty. Moving ever-soslightly. At the end of the rusty chains. In the light breeze.

I remember standing at the door. Knocking. Ringing the doorbell. Feeling like an intruder as I turned the knob. Walked through the doorway. And made my way into my childhood home. I called Dad's name. But the only answer I received was that old, familiar sinking sensation. The one that tugged at my insides. Threatened to pull me under. Take me back to the day that Mom died. When I'd been doing my duty as the good son. Checking in on her, as I always did when Dad was gone. Working overtime. Or away on a hunting trip. Or fishing. As was the case this time. With his fly rod and creel. After trout in the Fox River. Up US 23 North. Over the Mackinac Bridge. In Seney. Miles away from his wife and his home. And I came into the house. After knocking and ringing. And I called *her* name. Wondered where *she* was. And ended up standing outside the bathroom. Pounding on the locked door. Panicking enough to break it from its hinges and find her. My Mom. On the bathroom floor. Pants around her ankles. Eyes open. Seeing nothing. Face so blue it looked black.

And so I was at it again. But this time, I was outside my Dad's bedroom door. Wondering what waited on the other side.

A heart attack taking his color.

A stroke nailing him to the floor.

Something lasting and permanent. Hard to digest and dissolve. Another part of the family, another part of me, put to sleep in Pilgrim's Rest Cemetery.

But when I opened the door, Dad was there. Curled up. In the big bed that he and Mom had shared. That I had shared. With both of them. When I was just a kid. Wanting to be close. To keep away the autumn cold. Winter's loneliness. Spring's bad dreams. And the spooky reach of thunder and lightning on stormy summer nights. When all I needed was just a little human touch. The same thing that Dad seemed to need. As he rested now. In the big bed with the knotty pine headboard, the queen size mattress, and white cotton sheets. The whole of it growing bigger and bigger by the day. Cradling him. In his red pajamas. As he wandered about in dream. Away from the world. Safe in sleep. Mouth open wide. Air whistling in and out. Teetering on the edge of a snore.

The sight of him there. The soft rise and fall of his body, the way his eyes moved back-and-forth under the lids, made me feel good. Relieved. Like I'd been swimming underwater for minutes and finally allowed to break surface and breathe.

I reached to touch his face, to feel this sleeping man's cheek, because I couldn't remember ever doing it. But I stopped short. Pulled away my hand. Stood and looked around the room until my eyes came to something I'd never seen in the house before. A Bible. Next to Dad's alarm clock. On the night stand.

It was strange. Seeing a Bible there. In the bedroom. In the old house. Because even though Mom had been active in the church, organizing rummage sales, playing piano for the choir, my folks weren't particularly religious, and Dad had never attended services. Their literature was practical. Cookbooks. Encyclopedias. Dictionaries. *Newsday, McCall's,* and Dad's *Field & Stream.* There was a copy of the 1973 *Farmer's Almanac* and a Chilton's manual for every vehicle they'd ever owned, but as far as I'd known, there'd never been a Bible in the house.

I picked it up and opened it to a page that was book-marked with a *Chauncey's Bait and Tackle* receipt. Part of Psalm 6 was underlined with pencil.

Have mercy on me, O LORD, for I am weak: O LORD, heal me, for my bones are troubled.

Further down. Another part. Underlined in ink.

I am weary with my groaning: all night I make my bed swim: I drench my couch with my tears.

I looked over toward Dad. Imagined him alone at night. Reaching for Mom. Wanting to feel her. To hear her breathing by his side. But having nothing. No warmth. Only his own body sprawled out in empty space. Kicking away covers. Pulling the pillow over his head. Hiding away from the thoughts that come to a man at night. When he is so close to the dark. And so very far away from the morning light.

Dad sighed. Curled up tighter. Brought the pillow to his face.

I put the Bible on the night stand. Looked at the alarm clock and noticed the hands were dead. That time had stopped one day at 4:12 p.m.

Batteries, like every other odd and end, were kept in a kitchen cupboard. Duracells next to Wonder Bread. Shoe polish and RAID guarded spices and crackers. Fishing line and 3-in-1 oil mingled with meat tenderizer and vinegar. Jars of nuts and bolts and boxes of shotgun shells stood alongside cans of tuna fish, smoked oysters, and windmill cookies.

I was headed for the kitchen, with the intention of finding fresh batteries, when Dad came to life.

"Where are you going with my clock?"

"Needs new batteries," I said. "Don't you keep them in the kitchen?"

He stood in a rush. Grabbed the clock from my hands.

"The clock's fine," he said. And he put it back in its place next to the Bible.

"Go on and warm up the truck. I'll just be a minute getting dressed."

I turned and walked down the hallway, past the walls of family pictures. Our faces, moments, memories, lives captured and framed behind wood and glass. But I did not look at them. And I did not think about them. I moved quickly, away from Dad's lonely bedroom, the dead clock, the strange Bible, and I moved on through the kitchen, out of the house and got into the truck. I turned the key. Started the engine. I thought of the dead clock on Dad's night stand and finally it came to me. 4:12 P.M. was the coroner's best guess at Mom's time of death. And now, it was Dad's constant reminder.

Dad emerged from the house wearing his Sunday clothes. A red flannel shirt tucked into blue jeans. A baseball cap. His old Rocky hunting boots. And his trusty binoculars slung around his neck. He was staring into the sky as he walked around to the passenger side. And was pointing to something I couldn't see. I leaned forward. Looked heavenward, but couldn't see anything but big gray, flat-bottomed clouds stretching over the horizon.

Dad rounded the bumper, reached higher to point at whatever it was he could see, and he slipped and fell to the ground. I moved to get out of the truck. To help him. But he had righted himself just as quickly as he had gone down. He opened the door. Boosted himself onto the seat. Face flushed with color. Eyes beaming. He smiled as a broken V of geese moved overhead.

"Too early to be headed South," he said.

"You all right?"

"I'm fine. It's these damned boots that are causing the trouble."

He lifted one of his feet to show me the bottom of the boot. It was shiny and smooth. The tread long gone.

"Jesus, Dad. Maybe it's time for a new pair, hey?"

"Heck no," he said and he lowered the boot.

"Your Mom got me these for my birthday. They're great boots. They just need to be resoled. That's all."

Dad reached into his shirt pocket. Took out a can of Copenhagen. Opened it. Took a pinch. And raised it to his lips. Tobacco sprinkled his shirt. The rich smell wafted through the cab as he reached under his seat and pulled out a plastic Coke bottle. His makeshift spittoon for our rides. He crammed the bottle between his legs for safekeeping then took to the task of cleaning the binocular lenses with his shirttail. I put the truck in gear. And we started our drive.

It was October. Fields were changing. Green to brown. But the cows still grazed. Chewed slowly and stared. Big dark eyes unblinking as we passed and moved under a canopy of maples. Trees that had started the rationing. Slowed their growth. And were sacrificing leaves. Red, yellow, and orange. Signals of the season. The change. Floating, twirling, falling down, as we neared Mann's Corner.

Dad opened the Coke bottle. Spit inside.

"Did I ever tell you the story about Mom and why she thought they called it Mann's corner?" he asked.

"No," I lied.

Dad had started this some time ago. Shortly after Mom died. Bringing her back to life by making her a part of his everyday. In conversation. Shared anecdotes. Funny stories. Talking about her more when she was dead than when she was alive. But I understood then, as I do now, that this is what death does to us. It makes us want, and it makes us feel. So that we remember. Repeat and remain connected.

"Years ago, there was this accident," Dad began, as he always did. "Happened to a wedding party. Group of young kids just out of high school. It was December twenty-third. Two days before Christmas. I remember because we weren't having much of a winter and I was in the yard raking when I got the call."

Dad had changed a detail. The last time he had told the story, he was in the front yard, fixing some Christmas lights that would not blink. This particular time he was raking. But this was okay. It was good for him to remember creatively. To make things fit. Work. Make sense. And it was good for me because it kept me interested. Wanting more.

"Your mother was complaining about gravel that had been pushed into our yard by the plow trucks. Since it was the holidays, she was on high alert wanting everything to be just right for the company we were having. Relatives and friends that I never really cared to see. All coming over for a Christmas party, and Mom was worried that they'd see rocks in the lawn. It didn't matter that it was winter and that everyone was going to be inside eating, drinking, playing cards. Your Mom acted like people were going to be walking around barefoot in the yard."

Yes, Dad was changing the story. Winging it. But it still sounded like Mom, all right. Always wanting things to be just right in her immaculate home. Something she had taken great pride in. Clean and tidy. And always ready for visitors, even though the only company I ever remember were family members for holidays and Jake tromping into the house nearly every day.

I had seen pictures of other parties. Of another time. When I was still a notion. Something to come. A few of these photographs actually including me as something that didn't exist just yet. A bulge beneath a girl's dress. A pretty, slender girl that became my Mom. People I had come to know and people I'd never known surrounding her with their ears or hands near her belly. On the bulge. Patting it. Greeting me. Pictures with everyone drinking and smoking. Including Mom and Dad. Cigarettes dangling from mouths and held between fingers. Bottles and cans. Drinks in hands. Faces all smiles. People happy. Fit. Immortal. Innocent behind their glassy eyes. And our Home. A central character. Looking much less like a house and more like a bar or social club. Where everything was out of place. Scattered about. And nothing to indicate that being tidy, having a clean house would be the way Mom would want things to be.

"I ended up out there day before Christmas Eve," Dad

said. "Raking rocks out of a frozen lawn when all of the sudden it started to rain. Then light fluffy snow. And that's what did them kids in."

"The wedding party?" I asked.

"Yep. The whole group was heading to Long Rapids Chapel for the ceremony. The bride and her girlfriends were in one car. The groom and his boys were in another. The boys were following the girls and both cars were driving pretty fast. I guess they were playing around, you know. The girls trying to keep the bride out of sight. The old bad luck tradition. Anyhow, there's that sharp corner just before you get to the bridge, the place they put up that big power pole now, but apparently the girls didn't slow down. Had they hit that ice going the speed limit, the guardrail might have saved them. But they were really trucking along, probably excited, trying to get to the church and all. And when I got there, there were all these young fellas dressed up in tuxedos on the bridge.

The groom was hanging over the edge of the railing where the car had gone over into the river. He was screaming and crying and two of the groomsmen were holding him back. So he wouldn't jump over, I guess. It was like a bad dream. All those kids dressed up on their way to a wedding and ending up there on the bridge watching the bride and her girlfriends sink into the river."

Dad pauses. Takes a deep breath. It is my cue.

"Did they die?" I ask.

"The girls did. They all died. We found them all in the river that same day."

But then, a last new detail. An added touch.

"All except the bride. She wasn't found until spring. Hooked by a kid snagging suckers."

"Boy, that's a sad story, Dad."

"Sure is. But that's why your Mom thought they called it Mann's Corner. Because the girls died and the men survived."

When we got to the corner near the bridge, I slowed the truck to a crawl because the turn into the store's parking lot was tight and because I was trying to see something. To see anything that would make Dad's story real. Marks on the pavement. A bent guardrail. But there wasn't anything. Too much time had passed for there to be anything besides dead leaves and empty beer cans rolling around in the breeze.

The tank wasn't empty when we pulled into Mann's Corner. The gage was on the edge of full, but Dad said he wanted it filled anyway. He ambled into the store while I pumped gas. The pump was old as hell with rolling black-and-white digits, and although I barely squeezed in five dollar's worth, it took about five minutes. I gazed at the bridge and could hear the river moving along restlessly, eroding as much of the bank as it could before its course would be slowed by a season of ice floats and frozen debris. Though the sun was rising above the naked hardwood trees, it was barely visible because a veil of murky white sky was moving in.

When I removed the nozzle from the filler tube it dripped gasoline. Some of it splashed onto my shoes. The same shoes Mom got me in 2003, around Easter time. I watched the spots disappear. Some evaporated. Some seeped in. Maybe, I thought, I was the one who needed the new pair.

I heard Dad and Mr. Mann inside the store laughing. Carrying on as usual but their conversation halted as soon as I walked in. Mr. Mann's face was tight and fresh. His lips parted into a small smile. He had a shiny, bald head. As usual, I found myself staring at the place where fingers were missing from his right hand.

Dad had our bounty spread out on the counter in front him. Two bottles of Coke and a big bag of salt-and-vinegar chips. The cash register clinged and chinged, bells singing, as Mr. Mann pushed the clicking digits with the few good fingers on his hand.

When the total sprang up Mr. Mann nodded at me then winked at Dad.

"Five niney-nine, with your gas," he said.

Dad told him that we didn't need a bag. He scooped the goodies up into his arms. Handed me the Cokes. Told me not to shake them as we walked out of the store.

When we got to the truck I asked, "How'd he lose his

fingers, Dad?"

Dad stopped and looked back at the store.

"Hell if I know, but he's one of the best men I've ever met. I'd like him even if he didn't have toes."

We got into the Ford with the tank full up and our goodies in hand, and settled into the drive. Dad spat out his chew and tore into the chips. Took a handful then set the bag between us on the seat. He munched quietly. Mouth closed. Occasionally wiping his salty fingers on his pants. Crumbs fell all over and around him.

We moved slowly, between ten and twenty miles an hour, down Big Loop Road. An old dirt road that begins a few miles past Mann's Corner and circles The Ridge. A long, gravel stretch that's all stone farmhouses and hunting camps. Places you can't see from the road because of long winding driveways or fenced-in yards guarded by trees.

As we drove past a few off roads, trails and two-tracks, Dad pulled his gaze from the window and looked at me.

"Your Mom and I used to run these roads."

The Ford jumped over potholes. Shook us. I wanted to say something, but I didn't know what or how. This was something new.

Dad paused, as if searching through his mind for the right moment of memory, then continued.

"We used to hop into my old Chevelle, grab a case of Pabst, and just go riding. There's nice quiet places at the end of those trails."

"What did you do back there?" I asked.

Dad smiled.

"We'd sit and talk."

This wasn't true. I knew it wasn't true because down at the end of one of those grassy two-tracks is where I came into being. It is how I was put here. Action between two bodies. Not on a couch. Not in a bedroom. Not even during an impromptu hotel stay. But in the backseat of a '69 Chevelle. I had started as many things do, as basic desire. Hot lips. Rubbing hips. Fingers touching. Teeth biting. Grunts and groans. Two into one. One into another. A drip, a drop, a spark of light. An accident. Two teenagers. My Mom and Dad parked off the end of a grassy two-track. Coming together. Hot and in the dark and that is where I began. An upset stomach. A morning glow. A nagging urgency. Something growing in heart and mind. Something deep and moving. In a secret place. Inside her.

We were young and in love, Mom had told me time and time again.

"You know, Dad. I've been down some of those trails myself."

Dad looked out the window.

"Oh, I know. Believe me, I know."

"What do you mean?"

"You may've fooled Mom, but not me," he said.

My face burned. Fingers wrung the steering wheel. I felt caught. Like a kid again.

"That was my car you borrowed those nights. Coming back with mud and grass all underneath. Beer cans jammed under the seat. The interior smelling like perfume."

We laughed. And I drove. And I remembered driving those roads. Barely passable, wooded two-tracks, grassy and deep. Paths that led to wide-open fields and thick swamps. Places where people dumped bulging black garbage bags, unwanted furniture, and old washing machines.

Me and Beckie Milligan in Dad's car, drinking beer. Getting farther along with each empty can. Sweaty groping behind steamy windows. Pulses winding up. Time disappearing. All of it ending more suddenly and awkwardly than we could have imagined. Two creatures trying hard to find a way. To grow. To love. To learn. To save what we had because we were young and afraid of losing it. Of losing us. Coming apart because that's what we were supposed to do. Beckie moved away and moved on. Found other roads to travel. Other men to love. Other places to grow. I stayed. Parts of me were able to move on within the confines of this small town. But other parts started to die. And the bitch about dying young is that you don't think of it. You cannot recognize it because you are thinking of *now* and how now adds up to nothing. And when there is nothing, there is no use in caring for tomorrow.

So then, what it takes is something special. Like finding your Mom. Dead on the bathroom floor. And being sent into blind desperation. It is secret and stifling. You cannot talk about it. You cannot confront it. So you dismiss dreams. Settle into routine. And begin the all-American, small town descent into comfortable self destruction. You do what you can to get by. To keep quiet. Make peace. Drift off into the other side. Even if that means drinking too much too often and being nudged by guilt and regret so that you wake early on Sunday mornings to drive the back roads with your Dad.

The only traffic me and Dad see on our last Sunday drive is the Talbott family. On their way to church, they pass us at Mustang Swamp, the lowest part of the road where the cedar trees loom over and make a shadow over the world. The Talbotts whizz by. All of them waving. Their Chevy Suburban tossing gravel and stirring dust so that it's like we've driven into the middle of a mini tornado.

Dad shakes his head. Grumbles under his breath. Calls them *assholes for driving so goddamned fast, on Sunday of all days*. Then shifts his attention to the world beyond his window. He gazes up into the sky. Watches it as we emerge from the dark canopy of trees. And I wonder what he's thinking about.

What he's seeing. What he's searching for and what there is to find in the big sky that is evolving, ever-so-slowly, into a mass of hanging gray.

We roll up alongside a wide sprawling field. One of the few places on The Ridge where we don't know the owner of the property. Dad has told me that he's heard it's a General Motors executive from Bloomington Hills. A rich fella that comes up with a bunch of his white collar buddies. To The Ridge. To hunt deer. For two sacred weeks in November each year. They have a two-story log cabin on a hundred and twenty-acre parcel that is split in half by the river. They have a bar, a sauna, two pool tables, and a hired cook. That's what Mr. Mann has told Dad, anyway. And that's what Dad has told me.

Dad motions for me to stop. He gets out his Copenhagen and takes another dip.

There is a rock pile in the center of the field about two hundred yards out. There are deer grazing near it. Dad raises the binoculars. Tries to steady his hands so that he can find them in the lenses. And it is strange seeing him like this. Deep wrinkles, hands trembling, hair dusted with gray.

"Two does," he finally says. "And one looks like a yearling."

He hands the binoculars to me. Everything is blurry so I adjust the lenses for my eyes. I see the does, but see something else too. A dark, thick-shouldered buck with eight points worth of tines.

Dad lifts his Coke to his lips, unscrews the cap, and instead of taking a drink, spits into it. When he puts the cap on he realizes what he's done.

"I just spit in my pop."

"You want mine?" I ask, as I hand him the binoculars.

He shakes his head. No.

Dad raises the glasses, adjusts the lenses and takes another look. I grip the wheel and bite my tongue. Hold my breath in silence and wait. I wonder if he's seeing it. I want him to see it because I know that's what we've been looking for. I want to hear him say that he sees it. That it's all muscles and antlers. And that its dark coat means one thing. That we are in for an early winter.

"You better take another look," he says, as he turns away from the window, smiling.

He hands the binoculars back to me.

"Did you see it?" I ask.

"I sure did," he says.

But I'm not sure he has. So I put the binoculars to my eyes, adjust them, and I'm amazed when I see nothing. The field is gray and brown. Stiff, dead grass wavers in the wind. A crow flies and lands on the rock pile. I see the hardwoods in the distance. Colors bleeding away. And I see the sun behind it all, trying to reach us, but the deer are gone away.

✿

By the time I reach The Ridge and pass the house I grew up in, I am exhausted and confused. Full up with memory. Mom and Dad are dead and gone. The old house, the wraparound porch, the swing are all there, but I refuse to see them. Instead, I focus on Jake as he waits by the road. Fishing rod. Net. Tackle box. And a case of beer under his arm.

I stop. He throws the gear into the truck bed. Opens the passenger side door. Jumps in and buckles the beer safely into the seat between us.

"After last night, we can't be too careful," he says, and he gives the beer a loving pat.

"They weren't Greek by the way."

"What?"

"Mann's Corner. Those weren't Greek girls."

"Oh, I know. I heard the real story this morning on the radio."

"So where'd you get your information?"

"Truman."

"The bottle-picker?"

"The one and only. He was at the creek."

"In the middle of the night?"

"He says he makes a killing when the suckers run. Guys leave bottles and cans all over the place. Fishing and drinking go hand-in-hand, you know."

He gives the beer another little pat.

"How'd he do last night?"

"Not so good. I was the only one out there and I didn't drink much. But we talked awhile and I gave him my empties. I think he felt obligated to give me something in return, so he made up that story."

"He got some of it right. There were two girls in an accident."

"A busted clock is right at least twice a day," Jake says.

And I think of Dad's clock. In the empty old house. On the night stand, near the bed. Hands still stuck at 4:12 P.M.

As we roll away, I glance in the rearview mirror and I can see my Dad at the end of our old driveway. The hangover, the drive to The Ridge, my wandering mind and memory have all conjured him so that he is alive and well. Wearing his red flannel shirt. Blue jeans. And work boots. Waiting for his son to take him for a ride.

"The suckers aren't running," Jake says. "We need rain. A good thunderstorm will bring 'em in."

I drive. Jake looks ahead. Up at the sky.

"Think Kali's still sleeping?" I ask.

"She's sleeping all right."

"How do you know?"

"She's on my couch," he says.

There's a surge of something inside of me. It is not

jealousy. It is not excitement. But it is warm. Like the pull from a whiskey bottle. The sight of a shooting star. Or that familiar feeling—the slight tug of a fish at the end of your line.

Jake smiles. Takes two bottles from the case.

"It's beer-thirty," he says.

"I don't know if I can drink one yet."

Jake takes this opportunity to tease me. Make fun. His backwards way of showing he cares.

"Poor baby got a sour stomach?"

I take the beer. Open it. And I am surprised at how good it feels. Refreshing and cold as it goes down.

"Delicious!" I say. "Just what I needed."

"I bet. After the amount of alcohol you consumed last night, I'm surprised you're still standing."

"I'll always be standing."

"Sure *you* will. But poor Kali was tanked," Jake says. "I couldn't let her drive and she didn't want to go home."

I reach for the radio. Some distraction, but Jake swats my hand.

"No radio," he says.

"Why not?"

"Sooner or later you have to talk about it, Aden."

"There's nothing to talk about."

"I didn't think so either. Until last night, I thought it was just another case of lonely boy meets lonely girl. They get drunk, fuck, and fall in love, stick it out as long as they can, then part. But now, I know that's not the case."

"What did she say?"

"She talked about a baby, Aden. And about all the plans. But that can't be, can it?"

I am silent because there is nothing I can say. We ride along, drinking. And we are quiet for a time. Searching the familiar scenery of Pilgrim's Bay for the flash of something new. But the only newness we have is this awkwardness of a secret let loose between friends. I do not want to speak of it, or think of it, and I do not want to fish the dam. But I am too hungover and too tired to fight. And it is much too late to turn around.

"I'm sorry," Jake says. "I know Kali makes you sore. I shouldn't have said anything. I'm sure you already got enough on your mind."

"What else is on my mind, Jake?"

"You know. The day and all."

"What day?"

"Today. It would have been your old man's birthday."

My stomach turns. I grip the wheel. Fight what's rising inside. And I can't believe that all moments have led to this. Driving to pick up Jake to fish the Ninth Street Dam. Thinking all the while of my Dad, but not knowing enough to remember his birthday, or to remember how old he would have been. And then the secret let out. To live and breathe. Even though I believed it would only belong to me. And to Kali. That it would always only belong to us. To be ours. To have and to hold. And so, the weight of everything tugs and pulls. Creates uneasy silence in the cab of the truck as we ride along to the dam. And even though we wave and nod at people who are out and about. Riding bikes. Walking dogs. Jogging. Our only exchange is when we hit the bottom of our bottles and Jake takes two more from the case.

"It'll be okay," he says.

I don't say anything. Jake turns and stares out the window. I fight to stay distracted by details on the surface.

A big new sign at the funeral home and new asphalt in the driveway under the wheels of the funeral home director's brilliant white, customized SUV. Tinted windows. Gold trim. Vanity plate that says PRLY G8S.

Teenage girls at the entrance of the AUTO SPARKLE CLEAN. Dressed in cheerleader uniforms. Bouncing around with pom poms. Holding cardboard signs. Begging for motorists to stop and get their cars washed. So that they can fund their trips to away games.

A young woman. Looking much like Kali. Beautiful and perfect in her sweat pants, long sleeves and sneakers. Dark hair pulled back into a pony tail. Pushing a pink baby stroller that has chubby little arms reaching out toward the sky. And I am touched. Pushed beneath the surface. Into a place in my past that I cannot believe is mine.

✿

We had planned it. All of it. Best dates to conceive. Best months to give birth. What to eat. Drink. How to sleep. Colors to be used in remodeling the spare bedroom. What to listen to. Watch for. Feel. And as quickly as we had put ourselves into it, we were pulled out.

Jake and I were at Sammy's. Drinking beer. Shooting pool. It was the most sober I'd ever been. Because Kali and I had made a deal. She could not drink so I would only drink once a week. On Wednesday nights.

"How's she feeling?" Jake asked.

I racked the balls.

"Not good. Lots of cramping. Feverish. She's been in bed for two days."

"What did the doc say?"

"It's Pilgrim's Bay General," I said. "What do you think?"

"I think that if I went in there with a gunshot wound to the head, they'd pack me full of cotton balls and send me home."

"That's about right. They told her that it's nerves. Stress. That she needs to relax. Get off her feet."

Jake slammed his stick into the cue ball. Put in three solids on the break. We'd already had two pitchers of beer, so we were loose and our games were getting better.

I poured the last of the beer into our glasses. Held the pitcher up into the air and waved it at Sammy.

"More aiming fluid!" I called to him.

But Sammy was on the phone. Talking. Motioning for me to come over.

I knew then that it was Kali. But I was not worried for she had called Sammy's before. Sometimes the simple question, *when will you be home?* Other times a special request, *can you ask Sammy to fry up a batch of mozzarella sticks and bring them home to me?* And even a few other times, *I just wanted to say goodnight since I'll be asleep soon.*

"She sounds real bad," Sammy said. And he looked worried when he handed me the phone.

There was a soft waver to her voice. She sounded tired and small.

"There's something wrong," she said.

"Are you okay?"

"No, Aden."

"Do you need me to bring anything?"

And the soft waver gave way and she cried.

"Aden...I...I need you to come home."

I drove through the dying day as the light gave way to dark and the defroster and heater did nothing to stave off the cold that eased into my bones. Down deep in my gut I felt as if something had gone missing. That everything had changed and would be different because there was a growing, gaping hole. One that could never be filled. And would always be waiting. For us to recognize. Acknowledge. Hold.

When I got home, Kali was in the living room. On the rocking chair. Naked from the waist down. Knees pulled up to her chin. Red fingerprints stained into the back of her thighs.

I moved to touch her, but she pulled away and she fixed her eyes on the bloody towel that was on the floor. In front of the flames that flickered in the woodstove.

"I didn't know what to do," she said. "But I thought I should keep it warm."

☼

"You all right?"

Jake asks this as the truck comes to a stop in the parking lot next to Chauncey's Bait and Tackle. The river is high and rushing white through the dam.

"We made it," I answer, but I can barely remember the drive.

We gather our fishing gear and the beer. Cross the broken sidewalk and take the dirt path that leads to the shore under the bridge. The trees are chalky gray. Limbs are bony black fingers reaching into the blue sky. The sun shimmers on the river.

Three of the dam chutes are open. Water rushes and froths. Breaks against rocks in the shallows. Becomes swirling glass in the deep. At the river's edge, there are fish bones, fish heads, discarded leaders and lines, beer bottles, candy wrappers, and pop cans. The houses on the opposite riverbank tower and stare. Cars rumble and thump over the Ninth Street Bridge. In the sun they are silver streaks of light flashing by.

Two men in a small aluminum boat are anchored near the bridge, drinking beer and fishing.

"There's a good hole there," Jake says.

"They're over one of the wrecks."

"Plenty of wrecks down there," Jake says, leaning over and looking into the water.

"Too many," I add.

I watch the river. Look out over the bay toward Lake Huron. And I wonder if I'll be next. Wrecked or drown. Following in my Dad's wake. One day. Because I've gone too far. Alone in an old boat. In water that's too rough. Under skies that threaten. But because I am so filled up on beer and good fishing it is impossible to turn back, to take shelter. Because I know I have been drunker and that the waves have rolled higher, and that I have been through much more than this. That I've seen storms come over the bay. Come over me. And I have always made it through. And I imagine that I'll make it through more, so I move ahead with lines in tow, into waves that are rising with heavy, gray sheets of rain beating down. Until suddenly, I hit the big fish. So big that it pulls and fights and makes the storm disappear and the boat drifts off course, but because I am so sure of where I am, where I am going, that I know how to get back, I reel instead of worry, and stand too close to the edge like I've done hundreds of times, but this time I slip. Fall. And all at once, I am part of it. Senses are washed by cold water. Blackness rolls in. And there is nothing I can do. The boat is moving. Waves are pounding. My arms and legs are heavy, and no matter how much I fight, I sink like every living thing eventually does. And I die. All alone in familiar territory. With the knowledge that I'll never be found. That there'll never be an ending. That I am only another distracted man. Drunk in an old boat. In a storm I cannot conquer.

And I remember how we spent two days trolling the river and the bay in Jake's boat. Dragging giant homemade treble hooks through the deep because I wanted to be the one that found him. To bring him back to the surface. Back into the world. Even if it meant learning the final, definitive answer. That my Dad was dead because he had drowned. Like so many other men.

We hooked rocks and wrecks. Logs and furniture. But we never hooked into my Dad. Jake hauled up an old bicycle that he kept, refurbished, and rode once before leaving it to hang from the rafters of his garage. I pulled up a roll of old carpet that had a .30/.30 rifle hidden inside. But I threw it back. And we watched it sink. Both of us in agreement that some things are better left alone. At the bottom. To rust and rot away.

"Do you think they'll ever find him?" Jake asks.

"I don't know. Part of me believes he wanted it this way."

"It's a hard way to go."

"It is, but I think he went out the way that he wanted to."

"Nothing wrong with that," Jake says.

"Nothing at all."

"How do you want to go, Aden?"

"I don't know," I say. "But I hope I don't take anyone with me."

"We all take somebody with us," Jake says.

And then, almost as an afterthought, he says, "I think I'll drown one day. I dream about it sometimes. Being at my own funeral. Seeing you and Kali and your Mom and Dad. Even Sammy and Truman are there. And my body is in a casket full of water and my face is bloated and blue."

"You're dead and at your own funeral?" I ask.

"How else would I be there?" he says. And I wait for the crooked smile and the laughter, but it does not come.

The sound of the water against itself, against the rocks and against the bridge pillars is soothing. Me and Jake rig our lines. Steel leaders. Split shots. Hooks. Jake takes a small coffee jar from his tackle box and unscrews the cap. Hands me a squirming, icy-cold nightcrawler.

"What are we going for?" I ask.

"Hungry fish," he says.

Jake threads a crawler onto his hook. Slings the line into the water. I bait mine. Toss it into the river. The crawler is pulled under. The line tightens. Straightens away into the current. Slices the surface like a translucent vein. And the small struggle begins. I cannot see it, but I feel it. The crawler and split shot tagging along the river bottom. Rolling through rocks and weeds, lost line and lures. Tapping along the bottom, exploring the deep.

I bend over. Put my hands into the cold water. Rinse them clean. And a chill runs through me.

Jake's stuck the case of beer into a hollow spot in the riverbank. He takes out two bottles. Hands one to me.

I dry my hands on my shirttail. Take the beer. Then stand holding the rod.

"You're old man got me using crawlers," Jake says.

"I like lures," I say. "More action."

Jake smiles, raises his beer to toast the sky.

"'*Lures are for sissies*!' That's what he used to say."

I raise my bottle, "Lures *are* for sissies."

"That makes you a sissy," he adds.

"It sure does," I say.

And we clank our bottles together and drink.

We go through several beers and all I keep thinking about is how it's Dad's birthday. How if he were alive, he'd be with us. Beside me. Talking about the river and how it used to be. Before there were seven chutes. When the bridge was wooden. When the shores were lined with fathers and sons, day and night, fishing for steel head, or snagging suckers. Catching whatever they could to take home to ice boxes, frying pans, smokehouses, and ovens. And Dad always knew what was down deep. Under the surface. Where men fished. A piano. A fish shanty. A car. And there'd always be a story. True or not. And it would mesmerize me.

For a moment, I can sense him next to me. Smell his chewing tobacco in the breeze. And it's like he's risen from the deep, swam upstream, and he's standing next to me. Waiting. But when I turn to see him, it is only Jake. He has opened a can of Copenhagen and is stuffing his lip with chew.

"I thought you quit."

"I did. But it's a special occasion."

He holds the can toward me.

"Want some?"

I shake my head. Turn away.

The men in the aluminum boat that are anchored over the wreck catch a silver-gray sucker. Its white belly shines in the sunlight. Before they can unhook it from the line, it falls into the boat. They scramble after it. The boat rocks. And part of me hopes they tip over. That they are taken by the deep. That maybe by sacrificing them, I will get my Dad back. Get myself back. But the boat settles. And one of the men grabs the fish. Holds it tightly and beats it against the side of the boat until it is dead. Then he throws the fish onto the shore. Seagulls rise up from all around, sweep down and race toward it. The largest bird claims it. Spreads his wings, lowers his head and calls from deep within his breast. Staking claim to the world.

"If Dad caught a sucker while we were trout fishing he would beat it against a rock or a log and then throw it onto the shore."

"Gotta keep things pure," Jake says. And he spits into the river.

The men in the boat pull up anchor and motor away. In their wake, a big fish rises, breaks the surface and splashes in the light of the sun.

The alarm on the dam sounds. A warning. A signal. If you are in the water get out. Chutes will be opening. More water will be coming. The current doesn't care about you. It will knock you off your feet. Fill your waders. Soak your clothes. Water-log your lungs. It will consume you. Sink you and bounce you downstream to the mighty Lake Huron. But before you're gone, before you're part of the dead men, hungry fish, lost lures and line, you'll be given one last image. A vision. Something to take with you. To the other side.

Like the big blue water tower bending and shaking through the water's surface. Flat and menacing against the sky. Peering down at you like a monster. So that you will know it and feel it and you will recognize it when finally you are absorbed. Part of it. In its guts. Saved up. Stored. Something to feed the lawn. Wash the car. Put out the fire. Bring flowers from the ground.

Like white curtains closing over a tall narrow window in one of the old riverbank houses. Eyes looking out, seeing the day, a bird, a car on the street. Seeing you as you slip into the deep, but seeing is something that cannot be believed so the curtains are closed and life goes on.

Like the Saint Paul steeple, three dimensional and glowing bright in the smooth, blue sky. A beacon of hope. Something to hold onto as you take one last look toward land and you see your fishing buddy on the bank, running alongside of you, panic in his eyes, stumbling, tripping over jagged rock, falling as you fall, his body hitting the ground as yours is swirled and churned away into the darkest, deepest cold spot. And the light disappears.

And I wonder to myself. What did *he* see? If anything at all.

"It's getting dark," Jake says. "Let's reel in."

We haven't caught anything. The air has gone cold. The

sun is useless as it winds down for the day.

"We got nothing."

Jake drains his beer, shakes his head.

"No. We got cold. We got air. And I don't know about you, but I got a buzz."

All chutes open. Water rushes hard so it's difficult to hear.

"*Sammy's?*" I shout.

"*Sammy's!*" Jake shouts back.

We walk up the path toward Chauncey's. There's paper stuck under my windshield wiper, flapping in the breeze. Tick-tick-ticking against the glass.

AT SAMMY'S. COME JOIN. DRINKS ON ME.

~ KALI

I hand the note to Jake. He reads it aloud. And smiles.

"She still loves you," he says. And he gets into the truck and closes the door.

I stand outside and listen to the river. Take deep breaths of the cold. Two mallards whistle through the air above. Sail over and follow the river to the place where it empties into the bay.

kali

Kali came at the end of June. The beginning of another fine Michigan summer. Weddings. Graduation parties. Sunshine. Warming waters. Pike and bass in Misery Bay, and Jake and I wrapping up days of work, of celebration, of every day, wading thigh-deep, casting over rock beds, alongside dead falls and near weeds. Fishing nearly every day. Like we had every summer of our lives since we were kids.

Then everything shifted. And in an instant the world changed. And I was holding Dad's hand. His rock-crushing grip. Tears down his cheeks. But I couldn't cry. Wouldn't cry. Because I was the anchor. I needed to hold tight. To be more.

I didn't listen to the reverend. I ignored sympathetic stares. Hugs. Condolences. None of it mattered. Silk-lined casket. Flowers. Biblical verse. People in suits and dresses. There because they had to be. Showing compassion. Shedding tears. And none of it meaning anything because Mom was dead and gone. Already part of another place. Moving on.

In the middle of the reverend's story of how Mom and Dad met and lived their happily married life—two of God's children coming together to do God's work (a story filled with inaccuracies and ignorance, all for the sake of the paraphrasing the teachings of Jesus)—Dad let go of my hand.

"I need a chew," he said. And he stood up to leave.

People gasped and murmured. But it was too late for appearances. For putting on a show. Mom was gone. We were all that was left and we knew it. So we walked outside and stood together in silence. A steady Lake Huron breeze pushed through the streets. Down the sidewalks. And whipped up around us.

Dad pulled a can of Copenhagen from his suit coat. His hands shook as he took a big pinch. Tobacco sprinkled and was blown away like dust as he raised it to his lips.

Jake emerged from the funeral home. Rubbing his red eyes. But doing his best not to make a mess. To make it worse. He put his arms around us. Pulled us close.

"She was such a good person," he said. "It doesn't seem fair that she's gone."

Jake wiped his nose and face with his sleeve. Dad dabbed at his eyes with a handkerchief. I stared into the sky. Watched white clouds sail over the big cross atop Saint Paul's Church.

"As soon as this is over," Dad said, "I want you guys to head out. Go fishing. Have a few beers. Blow off some steam."

"We can't leave you," I said.

"I'll be fine."

He looked over his shoulder at the funeral home.

"Especially after this is over."

"You sure you're gonna be okay?" Jake asked.

"Positive," he said, and he put his arm around me.

"*This* is the guy we gotta keep an eye on."

We stood outside for a long time. Talking about fishing.

Jake's woodworking. The rising price of gas. Everything except the matter at hand.

"We better head in," Dad said.

We returned to the funeral home. People lined up near the casket. Some cried. Some forced sad smiles. All of them stopped at the body. To remember. To forget. To touch her. To pray. And Dad and I sat there. Holding strong. Thanking people. Giving them closure. Helping them say goodbye.

After the funeral, me and Jake went to Sammy's. We sat down at the bar. Ordered two pitchers and waited for Sammy to bring them over.

"You all right?" Jake asked.

"Fine," I said. "Just thirsty."

Sammy came round.

"On the house," he said. "And I'll keep 'em coming as long as you need 'em."

I nodded. Sammy winked. Jake raised his glass to toast.

"I don't want to toast her," I said. "I just want to drink."

"Well, then here's to getting drunk," Jake said.

He touched his glass to mine and we started our way to the bottom.

Suddenly, the door opened. Light filtered through the smoky darkness. And a shadow walked in. I watched it shift and change, take on the form of a shapely young woman as she breezed into the room and sat at the bar next to me.

Long dark hair. Fair skin. Rosy cheeks. Dark eyes. And I could smell her. Just-showered. Spring fresh. Herbal and fruity. She ordered a sapphire and tonic. Sammy asked for her I.D.

She lit a cigarette. Pulled a book from her purse. Tuned out the world and began to read. Sammy gave her a clean ashtray. Served up her drink.

"Happy birthday," Sammy said to her. "First one's free."

Somewhere beyond this place, beyond smiling family portraits framed on home-sweet-home walls, beyond Mann's Corner and the Ninth Street Dam, beyond hungry fish, nightcrawlers, steeples, and caskets waiting for the ground, hands had set forth motion, action, scene. Coincidence and chance. Events. People. Bodies rushing toward each other, into or away from a center to meet, converge, and marry. To crash into power poles, meet in bars, and cry at funerals. Bodies seizing. Stopping. Coughing and choking. Ending on the cold tile floor, or in deep unforgiving water. So that life is changed. Never settled. A steady flow.

Kali had been born. Somewhere in the past. On the day my Mom was to be buried.

Music started. Somebody had changed the tune. Used fingers to put quarters into slots. Push buttons. Set the tone. Change the energy. Alternate the current. Move our moods. Bring it all together. For the day. For the night. For drinking. For an absence. And for grieving. Jim Morrison, breaking on through to the other side. And the other side was in front of me. A reflection of a world of people, of an existence that I did not believe would be. Everything flowing and fuzzy. Never to be clear. Nothing ever to be as it seems. Living from hangover to hangover. Lifting my feet, moving ahead day to day. Year to year. All of it the same.

I was staring straight into it. Seeing the beginning and end all at once in a smoky, red-eyed looking glass. And there she was. Looking up from her book. Staring into the same thing. Our eyes meeting in distorted reflection.

"Sammy, another drink for the birthday girl."

She smiled. Snubbed out her cigarette. Set the book aside.

Sammy brought the drink.

He smiled at me. Said to Kali, "Be nice to the kid. He's had a rough day."

She turned toward me.

"What's so rough?" she asked.

"My name's Aden," I said, and I offered my hand.

She put her small, warm hand into mine.

"Kali," she said.

"What are you reading?"

She put the book into her purse.

"You answer mine and I'll answer yours. What's so rough?"

Jake had been listening. Watching in the mirror. He smiled and loosened his tie. Sammy was listening too. Pouring himself a drink. I wanted to say it, but I wasn't sure if I could. Wasn't sure the dam would hold. But I had to test it and I had to know where I was headed.

"What's rough is that we buried my Mom today."

My throat tightened. And I felt it coming. So I picked up my drink and swallowed it down. My eyes watered. I stared into the beer. Tried to concentrate on the small bubbles rising from the bottom of the glass.

Jake put his hand on my shoulder.

"It *is* rough," he said. "But you're tough and you'll get through."

"Let's take a booth," I said.

Sammy rushed ahead of us. Wiped down the table and seats. Set out a clean ashtray. Me and Jake sat down. Sammy came back with more drinks.

"I'll keep an eye out," he said. "But if you need anything, just holler."

Sammy walked away. Poured a few drinks for the regulars that were huddled together at the end of the bar.

"What's he gonna do with this place when he dies?" I asked.

Jake leaned back into the booth. Looked around the room.

"Nothing."

"You don't think he'll leave it to his family?"

"What for? This is Sammy's. Once Sammy is gone, Sammy's is gone. It wouldn't be the same."

I was trying to get my mind off things. Trying to talk about something else. About Sammy. About this place that was Sammy's but ours as well. I was trying to fortify the dam. Get to work on making it as strong as I could. Cement the cracks. Strengthen the weak spots. But I couldn't help thinking of Dad. How he'd be left alone. With only me. And I felt like a little boy, his finger stuck in the dike, trying to save the world from flooding.

"I don't know how Dad's gonna do it," I said.

"Your Dad's a strong sonofabitch. He'll be fine."

"But mom was *it*."

"But Aden, he's got you."

"He does now," I said, and sort of regretted it. Not because Jake would understand—because I knew he couldn't—but because I knew that Dad would come to rely on me like he had relied on Mom. That my role as son had already changed. Morphed into something more when Mom died there, alone on the bathroom floor.

Jake looked over my shoulder. I could feel Kali approaching.

"Want me to tell her to leave?"

"No, it's fine," I said.

Jake got up and went to the bar. Kali sat beside me.

"Catcher in the Rye."

She pulled the book out of her purse and put it on the table.

"Everyone else has read it. I thought I should too."

"Where do the ducks go in the winter?" I asked.

"They fly south," she said.

"Guess you're not that far into the book."

"Oh, a bar room literary type, are you?"

"More bar room than literary."

She picked up the book. Fanned through the pages.

"It's a good book, but depressing."

"I think it's hopeful."

She set the book down. Considered it a moment. It was a small paperback. The cover was plain white with black block lettering. The corners were bent and worn.

"Holden," she said quietly. "Holden and hopeful. They sound similar. But the book is sad. Holden is sad. He's a confused little boy that doesn't want to grow up."

I watched her lips. Her cheeks. Liked the way the tip of her nose moved as she talked. *She is something*, I thought.

"I don't think it's that he doesn't want to grow up," I said, "I think it's that he doesn't want to be an adult."

"This town is full of Holdens," she said.

I looked around the place. Men hunched over the bar. Their bellies and love handles bulging beneath shirts. I could not hear them, but I knew that their talk amounted to the Detroit Tigers, fishing, the dying economy and the price of gas.

"I wish there were more Holdens," I said.

Kali put the book into her purse.

"Guess I'll have to finish it before I can say much more."

"You'll see about Holden when you read the passage about the ducks in the winter."

"Are you okay?" Kali asked.

"Ducks in the winter," I said.

We were silent for a short while, but the bar was not. It was louder. I could feel myself filling up with sound and was not sure I could take much more.

"How much have you had to drink?" Kali asked.

"Not enough."

She lit a cigarette. Pulled the ashtray toward her. It was only then that I noticed the ring on her hand.

"You married?"

She blew a long, wispy line of smoke from her lips. Put her fingers in her hair and twirled curls.

"It's my mom's. I've been wearing it since she died."

"Hard to meet guys when you're wearing a wedding ring, isn't it?"

She smiled. Something stirred. Comfort. Like being

touched by someone who knew.

"You'd be surprised," she said.

Jake came back to the table. A round of shots. More beer. More talk.

Kali had lost her parents. Both of them. In a car accident. Killed by a drunk driver as they headed home from a matinee on a Saturday afternoon that was their twenty-third wedding anniversary. Kali was devastated, but tied up loose ends as quickly as possible. She threw a dart at a map and moved to Pilgrim's Bay on a whim. She had an inheritance, cashed in insurance policies, and decided she was going to live modestly for the rest of her life. She wanted to read, to learn, to know herself, she said. And when she got to Pilgrim's Bay she was glad because besides fishing and drinking, there wasn't anything else to do but be alone.

"You shouldn't be drinking so much," she said. "It'll only make it worse."

"There's no worse," I said. "This is as bad as it gets."

"Tomorrow you'll be closer to feeling better."

"I don't care much for tomorrow. Tomorrow is useless. It's all useless."

"Nothing's useless," Jake said. "Everything happens for a reason."

"That's not true."

I poured another drink down my throat.

"It's not true and you know it and I know it and Sammy knows it and Kali knows it and God knows it..."

"It *is* true," Jake said. "And God does know it. And you'll know it too. This too shall pass. You'll get through."

I looked around the place. More regulars had taken seats at the bar. They were laughing. Talking. Carrying on. Sammy served them drinks. Emptied ashtrays. Set out bowls of popcorn and peanuts. Everyone looked happy. And everyone was loud. Occasionally, one of them would turn, look over their shoulder and nod in my direction.

"Even they know," I said. "Those fucking guys know. Day after day they work their shifts, get bad lungs, bad ears, bad backs, and they get closer and closer to nothing. Pay more bills. Drink more beer. And get closer to nothing. And that's where we're headed too."

Kali stood up. Took my arm.

"To the jukebox," she said.

And in all of it I remember this–her long silky curls hanging in front her face and her hand on my arm as we flipped through the songs–and I wondered if it was true that men marry women like their mothers.

☼

For nearly her whole life my Mom had long hair. The reason for this was because Dad liked it long. When he'd met her she'd had long brown hair, and Dad—not being one for change—didn't want his wife to change. So my Mom, doing all she could for most of her life to please him, did not cut her hair short or attempt to change the style. It was always long, always brown, and nearly always straight. Except for those times when it was pulled back into a pony tail. Or curled for holidays and other special occasions.

She had finally decided to have it cut the day before she died. It was such a big deal that she had called me to talk about it.

"I'm doing it tomorrow while your Dad's gone fishing," she said.

"For all these years, I've had long hair. For him. But now, I'm getting older and I don't like messing with it. The brushing, the washing. It's a pain. Long hair is for young women and I'm not young anymore."

"You're still pretty young, Mom."

I pictured her reaching up, putting her hands on my cheeks, smiling. But it was only a picture. Something made up for me to remember as I sat there at my kitchen table polishing off a bottle of vodka. Talking on the telephone.

"You're not drinking, are you?"

I took a drink.

"No, ma'am."

"Good, you don't need to drink. It'll ruin you. Drinking

ruins everyone in this town, and you don't need to be ruined. And you tell that to Jake too. I get tired of hearing about your late nights. The drinking and driving. And the fights."

"I know, Mom."

"You know, but you don't know. Drinking will kill you. You'll end up wrapped around a tree, or pounded into the guardrail at Mann's Corner. Or one day you are going to fight someone who doesn't fight fair and get shot or stabbed and end up dead."

"Gee thanks, Mom."

"Well, I'm your mother. If I didn't care, I wouldn't say these things."

"Mom, I've gotta go. Jake'll be here soon."

"Where are you two going?"

"We're going to try fishing the break wall."

"Okay, but be careful. Seems every year we lose a few to the water and this year we're running behind."

"I'm always careful, Mom."

"Sure, like your Dad. I don't know why he can't at least call and let me know how he's doing. He's been fishing, gone away for two days, and he still hasn't called."

"Don't worry about Dad. He's an old buck. And he's always fine."

"You boys think everything is always fine."

"Okay, Mom. I gotta get going, but I'll be over tomorrow,

okay?"

"Tomorrow? What for?"

"To check in. See if you need anything. And to check out that new hairdo."

☼

Kali's hair brushed my arm.

"What do you want to hear?" she asked.

"Black by Pearl Jam," I said.

She looked at me. Into me. And she could see everything I'd ever done, thought, and said.

"Oh, Aden," she sighed, "you've been sad a long time."

the confession

Inside Sammy's. Kali is already drinking. And she is not alone. Maggie is with her. They have a booth and they are leaning across the table toward each other. Talking under the dim light.

"Your odds just increased," Jake says, as he slaps me on the back.

He turns and heads toward the bar. I walk to the booth. They are quiet. Kali is smiling. Maggie is not.

I stand near the table contemplating where to sit. Beside Kali or Maggie.

"Catch anything?" Maggie asks.

"Not a thing," I say.

"You always catch something," Kali says.

"I guess we caught cold. And a good buzz."

"What is it with Pilgrim's Bay and all of the drinking?" Maggie asks.

Kali and I look at each other. We know what it's all about and it is clear to me that Maggie does not know and could not know because it is something that some people cannot understand if they are not from this place.

"On that note," I add, "what's everyone drinking?"

"Jake's got it covered," Kali says. And I turn to see him coming toward us. Two pitchers of beer and Sammy following with a tray of frosty mugs and shot glasses brimming with something dangerously clear.

"Time for drownin' sorrows!" Jake shouts, as he places the pitchers on the table.

Sammy doles out the glasses and shots then hurries away to the line of regulars that is forming at the bar.

The girls rise from the booth.

"We'll be right back," Maggie says.

They walk away. Side-by-side. Like sisters.

Jake slides into the booth.

"Tonight's the night."

"For what?"

"For decisions to be made."

He nods at the jukebox. Maggie and Kali are there. Flipping through songs. Putting in change.

"You might as well sit your ass down and wait," Jake says.

"Wait for what?"

"For what's coming down the pipe. I have a feeling everything's coming to a head, Aden. I just hope you're ready for it."

I sit across from him. He sets the shots on the table at all four places. One for each one of us.

"Ready for what?"

"Coming to terms."

I pick up the shot. Toss it back.

"Hey!" Jake yells. "It's not time!"

"It's time, all right."

I pour beer for us.

"I couldn't tell you about it, Jake. I couldn't tell anyone."

"About what?"

"You know what."

"I know *I* know. But I need to hear you say it. *You* need to hear yourself say it."

A new song comes through the speaker above our heads. Something I've never heard before. Something upbeat. Synthesized. Untrue.

"Holy hell," Jake says. "Is that Britney Spears?"

I take a long drink. Jake drinks too. We sit for a moment. Just the two of us under the light. With smoke rising all around. Regulars coming in. Glasses coming together like church bells. And we listen to the song.

"That's not something Kali would play," I say.

"Aden, you *know* that Kali didn't play that. It was Maggie. You know that. Kali will start off with Joplin, move to Morrison, and then to satisfy *you* she will play Vedder."

"You know everything these days, don't you?"

"More than you think."

Jake smiles. I take another drink. The frost from the glass is cold on my hands. Melts. Runs down my wrist. Drips onto the table.

"You need to confess," Jake says.

"Confess to what?"

"Not to what, Aden, but to who."

"Then who, Jake? God? Kali? You?"

Jake leans toward me. I can see myself in his dark eyes.

"To yourself, Aden. Yourself."

Jake's prodding, my lack of good sleep, the drinking, and having Kali and Maggie together have made me edgy. I have never said it and I don't want to say it, but before I can stop myself, I slip and it is let loose to run.

"We had a baby but it died."

I say it, but I cannot say another word.

The girls are back. Kali sits beside me. Maggie stands near the table and is looking like she's got something very important to say.

"I can't stay," she says.

Jake and I are silent. Kali and Maggie exchange a look. As if they are old best friends that share secrets that nobody else can ever know.

"Why you leaving so soon?" Jake asks.

"It's actually quite late," Maggie says, and she looks off to the door that swings open, creaks, and closes as more people come in.

"We're just getting started," I say.

"That's what I'm afraid of," Maggie says. And she turns away and we are quiet as we watch her go. Through the thick dark crowd of warm bodies and blue gray smoke that hangs like fog in the dim light.

"And then there was one," Jake says.

Kali sips her drink. Moves closer to me. I can feel her leg. Her hip. Her arm against my side.

"You scared her off," I say.

"No, Aden. *I* didn't scare her off. You scared her off. And Jake scared her off. And the both of you will continue to scare people off until you realize that this is not a world that waits. This is not a world that is kind or forgiving, and this is not a world where people can survive on their own."

"I can!" Jake shouts, as he slams his hand onto the table. Grabs his glass and gulps the beer as if he is a man dying of thirst. His Adam's apple moves up and down like a piston. Beer drips down his chin. When his glass is empty, he fills it again.

Kali grabs her shot. Slides Maggie's over to me.

"You can't make it on your own, Jake. And you will find that out just as well as anybody."

Jake raises his glass. Winks at Kali. We drink the shots in unison.

"I've already made it," he says. "Everything else is a blessing."

"The more we fight and churn, the more blessings we receive," I say.

"What's that?" Kali asks.

"The more we fight and churn..."

"I heard you, but what is it? Some Eddie Vedder lyric? Some Jim Morrison poetry?"

"It belongs to somebody, I'm sure. Everything belongs to somebody. But for now, we'll call it an Aden and Jake drunkard original. Is that okay?"

"That's okay," Kali says. And she rises and moves to the bar. Empty shot glasses and empty pitcher in hand.

"The queen has emerged," Jake mumbles.

"Kali's no queen, Jake."

"You'll see. Just drink up, buddy. Just drink up."

The beer is cold on the lips, the tongue and the throat as it moves down the pipes into the gut and bathes the growing knot. I look around Sammy's. At the dark walls. The sports memorabilia, stuffed fish and deer, and mirrors and the dirty green floor and the pool tables and the regulars as they smoke and drink and eat and talk and smile and shout and frown, and I know only one thing. That I am tired. Tired of the dim lights. The smoky booths. The same old songs. And I want nothing else but to go home.

"More fun, my boys. Drink up!"

Kali has returned. A tray full of shots, frosty glasses, and two more pitchers of beer.

"That's an awful lot," Jake says.

"Too much?" Kali asks.

"It's never too much," I say, and we down the shots and fill our glasses and it continues this way for hours.

There is a point finally, as closing time rolls round, that I am too full to drink anymore. Jake is glassy eyed and red faced, and I feel as if I'm underwater. It is hard to see. Nearly impossible to hear. Sammy is at our table. Talking to Kali. It is time to pay the tab. Because I am drunk and because I feel it's my responsibility, I take my checkbook out of my back pocket and ask for a pen. Kali pulls one from her purse. Hands it to me. I fumble to open the checkbook, to find a check, and I struggle to write.

"This pen doesn't work," I say.

Kali reaches over. Takes off the cap.

"Are you going to make it?" she asks.

"I've already made it," I answer.

Jake laughs.

Sammy leans in and pushes my checkbook aside.

"No worries, Aden! We can square it away another day! You folks better get yourselves home."

"I'm goin' fishin'!" Jake pipes.

"You're not going fishing," Kali says.

"I'm goin' fishin' and Aden is goin' fishin'. Sammy, you wanna go fishin'?"

"Not today, Jake."

Sammy shakes his head. Pushes away the money that Kali has pulled from her purse. That she is trying to give.

☼

My head is against the cold linoleum. Arm slung around the base of the toilet.

The door opens. And the draft of cool air washes over me, but I don't move. My eyes are gone away into the black. Making shapes and forms on the back of my eyelids.

"Get up," she says.

It is Kali.

I am still.

"Get up," she says again. This time her voice is solid. Deep. And telling.

I don't move.

She kneels. Leans over me. I smell cigarettes and sweet alcohol on her breath.

"Aden."

Her hair brushes my face. Fingers trace my cheekbone.

I turn over to look at her. The room is so bright it hurts.

It is clear she's been crying. Her nose is red. Eyes bloodshot and smeared with mascara.

"He's gone," she says. And there is a great crack in her voice. And she shakes as she buries her face in my chest.

"Who's gone?"

Her tears soak my shirt. She pushes her body against mine as if she's trying to get inside.

"Truman found him."

"Found who?"

"Jake, Aden! Truman found him in the creek!"

It seems impossible. Absurd.

"But the creek isn't deep and Jake knows every inch by heart."

"He's gone, Aden."

"But he can't be. There must be some mistake."

"It's no mistake."

"But it can't be. The creek is so shallow."

"He fell off the end of the culvert, Aden. He hit his head and was knocked unconscious and he drowned."

There is a great rising inside of me. Kali holds me tighter. The room feels like it is growing bigger and bigger. Whiter and brighter. And it's as if we are a small lead shot fixed to a piece of broken line. Disappearing into the deepest part of the river.

<u>waking</u>

It is the phone that wakes me. But I don't want to deal with it. Not yet. So I stay in my place on the bathroom floor. Awake in the warm daylight that breaks through the blinds. Kali's head is still buried in my chest. Her ear is tuned to my heartbeat.

The phone rings and rings and rings. I think of my Dad. Leaving me one of those Saturday evening messages. I think of my last conversation with my Mom. I try to believe that losing them has prepared me for this, but it has not. Because living cannot prepare anyone for dying.

"We should go for a ride," Kali says.

"Should we?"

"Yes. Let's not stay in the house today."

The ringing stops. Only to start again.

"But we haven't showered and we haven't had anything to eat."

"We can be dirty and hungry for a while."

"Where should we go?"

"Let's get onto the road and go to wherever it leads."

"It might not lead far."

"Wherever it takes us is fine," she says. "But let's get away from the phone."

☼

In the truck. We are quiet. Listening to classic rock

music on the radio. Until the news of Jake's death sounds over the airwaves. Along with sports, weather, and stocks of area interest.

"Should I change it?" she asks.

"I don't know."

But it is too late. The broadcast has started and Jake's death is second in line. Right behind the news about the recent spike in gas prices.

Authorities have ruled it an accidental drowning. An early morning fishing accident in which alcohol was involved. Case closed. Time moves on. And before we know it, the news is over and Jimi Hendrix is singing about castles made of sand.

I'm feeling hot. Sweating out the hangover. Kali opens the window a crack. Lets the cool morning air flow into the cab.

She gazes out into a wide green field as we pass it. There are deer in it. Near a giant rock pile. And they are filling up on tall grasses and clover. Twitching ears. Swishing tails. Fattening up for the season to come.

"Are they always out there?" Kali asks.

"Always," I say.

We move down the road. Past sleeping houses with their sleepy windows and sleepy yards. And I imagine bodies in chairs. Watching morning television. Hands stuffing faces with bacon and eggs. Cereal and toast. Coffee, milk, hot cocoa, and orange juice. And I know that many of them are feeling the loss today. Looking at their custom-made cabinets, end tables and bookshelves, thinking of Jake. Contemplating the value of a handmade thing and how it can rise once the creator is dead.

For a moment, I feel the urge to drive to The Ridge. To Pilgrim's Bay Park. One of the places Jake and I had shared when we were boys. Where we caught sunfish and rock bass while wading the warm sandy shallows with cane poles, grubs and only a few feet of line. But the memories are too good. They are better left alone. And it is too soon to believe he's dead. So I stop short. And I turn left. Into Pilgrim's Rest Cemetery.

I open my window. Shut off the engine. And we sit for a moment. To watch the white sunlight flicker through the birch trees and evergreens. To listen to the chickadees call as they leap from tree to tree. And to hear the river gurgling as it rushes through the debris that used to be a beaver dam. The big maple at the back of the cemetery is full of green leaves that glint and shine as they shake and sway in the breeze. I feel Kali's hand on my arm.

"It's been a long time," she says.

We get out. And we walk. Hand in hand. Through rows and rows of headstones. Some glossy and new. Standing straight and tall. Others covered with scaly moss. Leaning sideways. Sunk into the ground. We stop at the markers of my parents' graves. The wind pushes. The leaves rattle. And I am glad I came. And that Kali is with me.

"It was raining the last time," she says.

"And lightning. That's why they called off the search, they said. The weather."

"It was a horrible storm, Aden. Remember? And you still wanted to come here."

"I needed to tell Mom that it was over. That we weren't going to look for him anymore."

We stand in silence. And I try. To comprehend. What it must be like. To go on. Underground. As part of the soil. The sun. The air. The sky. And for the first time in my life, I know that there's more here than stones with names. And I know that even when we have been separated by distance and time, we are together. Like fish in the river. Leaves on the trees. And sunlight in the sky.

Kali squeezes my hand. Moves closer. We walk past more stones. Names. Dates. The silly attempts at permanence we make. And it is comforting to know that none of it will last. Not the trees. The birds. The river. Or the sun. None of it. And because of this I am not scared, or ashamed, or saddened, as we walk toward the base of the great maple that guards the tiny lamb-shaped headstone that belongs to our son.

"I'm so sorry, Kali."

She pulls me close. We hold tight.

"I know, Aden," she says, "I know."

And all at once, she lets me in.